ELAINE CLAYTON

A BLUE RIBBON FOR SUGAR

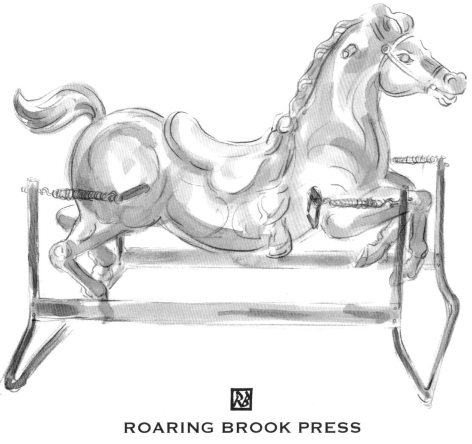

ROARING BROOK PRESS

NEW MILFORD, CONNECTICUT

For Alistair
And for Dad, who taught me how to ride

Special thanks to Jennifer Laros at Shallowbrook Farm for her help with this book.

Published by Roaring Brook Press
Roaring Brook Press is a division of Holtzbrinck Publishing Holdings Limited Partnership
143 West Street, New Milford, Connecticut 06776

Distributed in Canada by H. B. Fenn and Company Ltd.

Roaring Brook Press books are available for special promotions and premiums.
For details contact: Director of Special Markets, Holtzbrinck Publishers.

Library of Congress Cataloging-in-Publication Data
Clayton, Elaine.
A blue ribbon for Sugar / Elaine Clayton.— 1st ed.
p. cm.
Summary: After nearly wearing out her old hobby horse, Sugar, Bonnie learns how to ride a real pony and participates in her first horse show.
ISBN-13: 978-1-59643-157-7
ISBN-10: 1-59643-157-1
[1. Horsemanship—Fiction. 2. Ponies—Fiction. 3. Horse shows—Fiction.] I. Title.
PZ7.C57917Blu 2006
[E]—dc2   22005021909

First Edition May 2006
Book design by Tania Garcia
Printed in the United States of America
10 9 8 7 6 5 4 3 2 1

bridle An arrangement of straps that go over a horse's head, a bit that goes in the horse's mouth, and reins for the rider to hold.

cross ties Two posts, from which halters are attached to the horse's bridle, to keep it from walking away while being groomed or saddled.

flake A thin slice taken from the end of a bale of hay to feed a horse.

gait The way a horse moves, such as walk, trot, canter, and gallop.

girth The distance around a horse's middle. Also, the strap that goes around the horse to hold the saddle in place.

halter A rope attached to the bridle and used to lead a horse.

reins Leather straps attached to the bridle and held by the rider to steer and control the horse.

stirrups Rings hanging from both sides of the saddle that hold the rider's feet.

tack The gear (reins, bridle, saddle, etc.) used to equip a horse for riding. Tack is often kept in the tack room of a stable.

It was Monday morning. Bonnie was riding her pony, Sugar. She was the star cowgirl at the rodeo, whirling around the barrels, smooth as cotton candy around a paper cone.

She hurdled over fences, racing to win the steeplechase.

Bonnie was tossing a lasso over the neck of a young calf lost from its herd, when Sugar got spooked. He bucked and reared, popping a spring.

"Uh-oh," said her sister, Bridget. "You broke it."

Bonnie was not hurt, but her pony was smashed.
"It looks like this pony is ready to be put out to pasture,"
said Bonnie's mom.

"No," shouted Bonnie, stomping her feet. "Don't take Sugar away! He's my horse! Don't throw him in the trash!"

Bonnie was sent to her room for acting like a hot pepper in a frying pan.

For the next few days, Bonnie wandered around the backyard, feeling the sun bake the earth and listening to the wind whisper through the trees.

"Well howdy, Cowgirl!" said her neighbor, Mr. Woods. Bonnie could see the row of fence posts across the old farmer's forehead.

"I'm not a cowgirl anymore," said Bonnie.

"That's mighty sad," said Mr. Woods, his voice making a see-saw sound.

Mrs. Woods offered Bonnie a piece of her award-winning church fair cherry pie.

"I don't want pie," said Bonnie. "I just want Sugar back."

At breakfast on Saturday, Bonnie's dad said, "Get your boots on, Bonnie. We have somewhere to go."

"Can I come?" asked Bridget.

They drove up a dirt road past neat white fences and walked into a big barn. Their voices echoed as they spoke.

"This is Jennifer, your riding instructor," said Bonnie's dad.

"A real horse!" shrieked Bonnie. A shy-looking chestnut pony beside Jennifer lifted its head and backed up.

"Keep your voice low and quiet," said Jennifer. "Ponies get spooked easily."

"Oh, I know all about that," said Bonnie. "When they get spooked they buck! What is his name? Can I jump him over the rails?" Bonnie spoke fast.

"Hold on, Bonnie," said Jennifer. "His name is Burrito. He'll be your pony for each lesson. But we have to start at the beginning."

Jennifer led Bonnie into the tack room. There were bridles, halters, saddles, and blankets.

"These are for grooming," said Jennifer, pointing to the brushes.

Jennifer fitted Bonnie for a helmet of her own.

"Now let's ride!" Jennifer said.

She showed Bonnie how to get on the horse by using a mounting block.

Bonnie felt the girth of the horse beneath her. She smelled leather, dust, and horsehair.

"Hold onto your reins and keep your legs tight against the horse," said Jennifer. "And keep your heels down."

Burrito took a slow step or two, rocking gently forward. "I'm riding," Bonnie thought. "I'm on a real horse!"

Jennifer showed Bonnie the correct way to hold the reins.

"Keep your hands down," she said. "When you want to turn left, pull gently with the left rein and press your right leg into Burrito's side."

Burrito turned obediently to the left.

As the weeks passed, Bonnie learned to ask Burrito to walk at a quick pace. She felt Burrito's powerful gait and sat tall in the saddle.

She learned a seated trot, and then a rising trot.
"When you rise in your saddle with the rhythm of the
horse's strides, it's called posting," said Jennifer.

At the beginning of each lesson, Bonnie helped to tack up Burrito using the cross ties. She took the halter off and put on his bridle. Once the saddle was on securely, she tightened its girth.

At the end of each lesson, Bonnie brushed Burrito's hair, praised him for his hard work, and rewarded him with a carrot or a sugar cube.

The other riders taught Bonnie how to muck out a stall. "Gently shake the muck rake," they said. They taught her to feed Burrito a flake of hay.

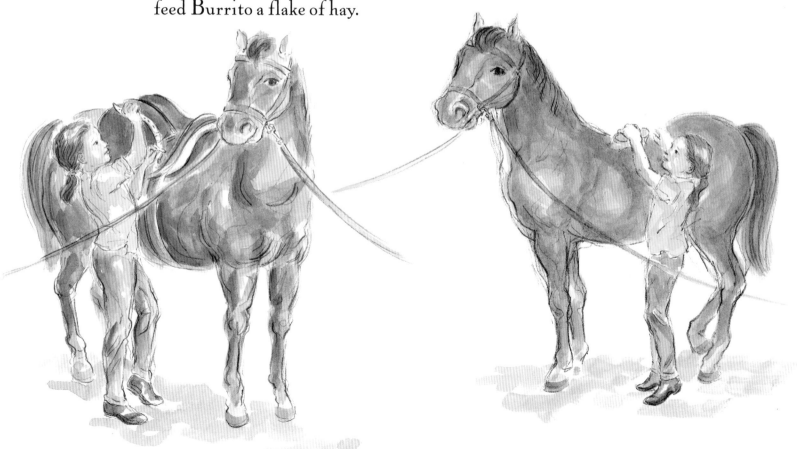

At summer's end, Bonnie took Burrito over a low cross rail.
Jennifer told Bonnie to put her weight down in the stirrups
and rise out of the saddle a little. "This will help you flow
with the horse's movements," she said.

"We jumped!" whispered Bonnie, giving Burrito a pat on
his broad neck.

On a sunny morning in August, an autumn breeze gently brushed Burrito's mane. Bonnie stood proudly beside him, his tail swishing. "Our first horse show together," Bonnie told him, patting his jaw. She knew he understood.

She also knew to be ready to have Burrito do whatever the judges asked of them.

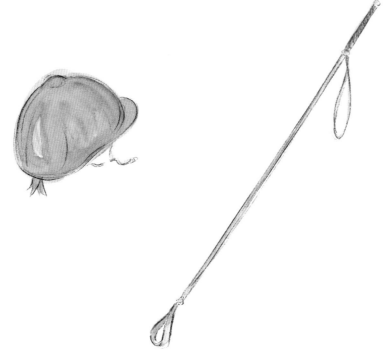

"Walk the ring, please," said a judge.
"And now trot around the ring."
Bonnie felt a happy twitching in her stomach as she rode.

Afterward, there was a ribbon ceremony.
"Excellent riding," said the judges.
Bonnie kissed Burrito, as she always did.
"You won this ribbon with me!" she said, giving
him a sugar cube.

At home, a celebratory cookout was planned. There were hot dogs and hamburgers, and Mrs. Woods brought her award-winning church fair cherry pie.

After they'd eaten, Mr. Woods said, "Little gals, I have a special somethin' for ya."

It was Sugar, fixed up like new again!

"I want to ride him!" said Bridget. She leaped on in one hop.

"Excellent riding, Bridget!" said Bonnie. "And a blue ribbon for Sugar!"